Tellwell Talent

www.tellwell.ca

ISBN

978-0-2288-5232-2 (Paperback)

This book is dedicated to my loves, Ryder and Rosie. Thank you to Samantha, Michele, Nina, and – as always – David and all members of my wonderful family.

Rosie Posie Lolly-Lu
had flame-red hair and eyes of blue.

She loved to paint, sing, and skip,
summersault, and backwards flip.

She'd sing out loudly in the mirror
and smile with pride from ear to ear.

Her mom took her aside and said,
"Share those thoughts inside your head."

After Rosie filled her in,
Mom cupped her hands round Rosie's chin.

"Just like your hair and eyes of blue,
your body was made just for you.

We all come in shapes of our own,
from our birth until we're grown.

Not just outside but inside too
are unique traits that make you ... YOU!

Like how you're kind, helpful, warm
and learned to flip with just one arm!

So Rosie Posie Lolly-Lu,
smiling through her eyes of blue,

rubbed her soft and squishy tummy,
and said, as she hugged her mommy:

"There's just one *me* under the sun,
a recipe used just for one.

I'm made just as I'm meant to be,
loved by others and, above all, me."

Back at school, she took a peek
and saw all bodies looked unique.

She noticed different curves and bends
on each and every one of her friends.

And she felt proud and grateful too
for all the things her body could do.

Like twist and stretch and lift with might,
jump and dance and hug real tight.

Years went by and Rosie grew older, taller, and stronger too.

One day at school, while eating lunch,
she took out ketchup chips to munch.

Her friend said in a not nice way,
"That's unhealthy – put it away.

If you eat junk food, which is bad,
you won't be strong, then you'll feel sad."

Rosie's cheeks then flushed bright red;
she wished that she could hide her head.

When she came home from school that day,
she didn't want to sing or play.

She felt ashamed and thought for long
about how she'd been eating wrong.

Her mom took her aside and said,
"Share those thoughts inside your head."

After Rosie filled her in,
Mom cupped her hands round Rosie's chin.

"There isn't food that's 'bad' or 'good';
foods are not 'shouldn't' or 'should.'

Eating healthy means finding a way
to balance different foods in your day.

To eat foods that build muscles and bones
and make you smile, like ice-cream cones.

Now Rosie Posie understood
that foods were neither bad nor good.

"Tonight, I'll eat hotdogs and rice,
green beans, grapes, and lemon ice!"

Then she smiled and hugged her mommy,
proud to feed and care for her tummy.

Rosie sat at lunch the next day
and said to her friend in a kind way:

"I've brought some chips and carrots too;
I'd love to share them both with you.

I've learned that foods aren't good or bad,
so now I feel relieved and glad."

And Rosie Posie Lolly-Lu
thought of this day as she grew.

And what her mom said years ago,
something that she'd always know:

"I am special and made just right,
no matter my size, shape, or height.

I love who I am through and through
and know that others love me too."

Years went by and Rosie grew
older, taller, and stronger too.

Then came the day she dreamed would come:
Rosie Posie became a mom!

Ryder Ray, she named her son,
who loved to skate, swim, and run.

With bright green eyes and flame-red hair
and freckles scattered everywhere.

When the bell had finally rung,
he left the class with his head hung.

At home, he didn't want to play
or chat like every other day.

Rosie took him aside and said,
"Share those thoughts inside your head."

After he filled Rosie in,
she cupped her hands round Ryder's chin.

She told him what HER mother said,
a message etched inside her head:

"Like your green eyes and freckles too,
your body was made just for you.

You are just right, inside and out,
and remember, without a doubt...

"You are so loved just as you are;
No one's more special, near or far."

CPSIA information can be obtained
at www.ICGtesting.com
Printed in the USA
BVHW061123291021
619988BV00002B/12